AMY'S DOLL

by Barbara Brenner
Publication date: April, 1963

Price: $2.79 net in reinforced
           GIBRALTAR binding
         $2.95 in cloth binding.

Will be of interest to: Children from Kinder-
                          garten through the 3rd
                          Grade.

Can be read by: Children in the middle
                          of the 2nd Grade.
                          (Spache Readability
                          Evaluation).

Curriculum: Reading. Family Life.

A delightful family story. Amy finds
the perfect old fashioned doll who goes
everywhere with her. The doll is lost,
finally found and renewed again at the
doll hospital.

AMY'S DOLL

by BARBARA BRENNER

photographs by SY KATZOFF

Alfred A. Knopf: New York

Our grateful thanks to *The Little Match Girl Shop*
and the *New York Doll Hospital,* for their
cooperation in the filming of *Amy's Doll.*

L. C. Catalog card number: 63-9101

THIS IS A BORZOI BOOK
PUBLISHED BY ALFRED A. KNOPF, INC.

AMY'S DOLL

Amy was seven years old.
She loved to play with dolls.

One Sunday Amy went for a walk. As she was walking she passed a store. She stopped to look in the window. And there it was. Sitting right next to a pink rabbit. There it was. The doll Amy had been looking for.

It was a beautiful old-fashioned doll wearing old-fashioned clothes. It had an old-fashioned wig and big brown eyes that could move. As soon as Amy saw it, she knew. That doll was meant to be hers.

Amy tried to go into the store. But the door was locked. She ran all the way home. Breathlessly she told her mother about the doll, and how much she wanted it. Amy told her mother how sure she was that the doll was meant to belong to her.

"Please may I buy it?" asked Amy.

"We'll see," said Mama.

That evening, Amy asked her father about the doll.

"Well—maybe," said Dad.

"My birthday is Wednesday," said Amy.

"Why, so it is," said Dad with a twinkle in his eye. "I had forgotten."

On Wednesday after school Mama suggested a little walk.

They walked right to that store. And Amy walked out with a wonderful surprise.

She could hardly wait to get home with her new child. A whole trunkful of clothes had come with the doll. Amy took off her outer coat and her dress. All the while she talked to the doll.

"Now what shall I call you, child? What is your name, anyway? Every child should have a name. I think I will call you—no—that's no good—how about—" Finally she said, "I've got it—Sarah Jane! That's what your name is—Sarah Jane!"

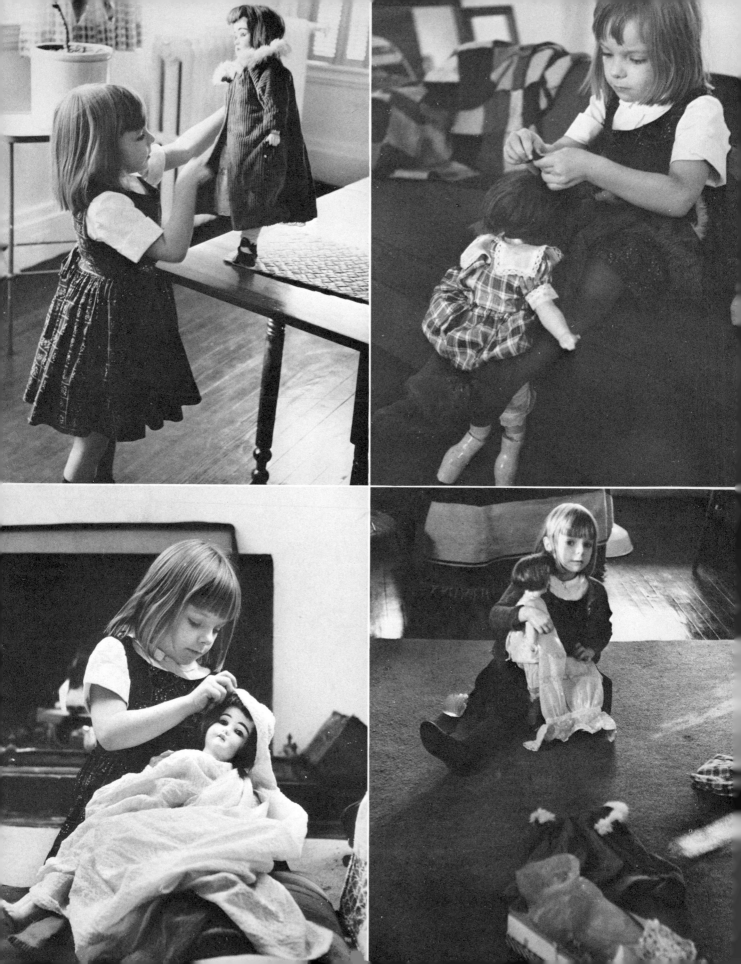

Amy dressed and undressed Sarah Jane seventeen times.

She showed Sarah Jane all around the house. Amy showed Sarah Jane the bed where she would sleep. Finally Mama called upstairs to say that supper was ready.

And when they went into the kitchen, Amy saw that Mama had set a place for Sarah Jane. And she met Amy's brother John who sat across from her at the table.

Now the new doll was part of the family.

Sarah Jane became Amy's favorite doll. She never said so, because the other dolls might feel hurt. But it was true. Sarah Jane was the favorite.

Whenever the children played secret games, or read to one another, it was Sarah Jane who was allowed to listen.

When Amy climbed trees, who was it who went along? Sarah Jane.

Sarah Jane went with Amy on trips to the attic and down into the basement.

Sarah Jane was the only doll who could touch the rock collection.

Sometimes Amy and Sarah Jane had a picnic in the garden.

Sometimes they took a walk together and looked for butterflies.

Once they even got sick together.
Sarah Jane didn't like to take medicine either.
"If you won't take your medicine, I won't read you a story."
"Changed your mind? That's a sensible girl."
"Open wide. Down it goes."

All that summer they were together—the girl and her doll. Then suddenly summer was over. One day the leaves began to fall off the trees. And by the time they were all off, it was winter.

Then———SNOW!

The children hurried into their heavy, outdoor clothes. Amy pulled a warm hat down over her ears. Amy's brother John wound a woolen scarf around his neck. Amy dressed Sarah Jane in her coat with the hood.

They all went out to play in the snow.

What a time they had! First they made a snowman. Then they went sleighriding.

Then there was a snowball fight. Snow down the neck. Rosy cheeks. Hide-and-seek. Cold noses.

Finally their hands were frozen. Their mittens were soaked. Their feet felt like ice inside their boots. And it was getting dark and blowy.

Amy and John and their cousin Alexander stood on the porch laughing and stamping their cold feet and blowing on their red hands. They brushed the snow off their clothes and dashed into the warm hall.

Flinging their clothes on the rack, they ran into the living room to sit in front of the warm fire.

They sat snug by the fire, watching the flames and telling stories. After a while Mama came in to sit with them.

"Tell me," Mama said, "did Sarah Jane enjoy her first snowstorm?"

Amy and John looked at each other. Sarah Jane! Where was Sarah Jane?

"You had her last!"

"No, you did. Remember I handed her to you to hold and—"

"I never had her."

Rush back into the soggy coats, the hats, the boots, the mittens. Rush back outside. Look for Sarah Jane.

But Sarah was nowhere to be found. They ran down the street. They looked behind bushes and in driveways and under sleds. They looked on the snow-covered bench. Everywhere.

Sarah Jane was gone. And it was beginning to snow again.

Slowly and sadly the children went home. Amy was crying. John said it wasn't his fault, it wasn't his doll. Mama was cross. Dad said he thought Amy had been careless. Amy cried harder and went to her room. Everyone in the house was upset.

While somewhere outside the snow fell on the lost doll. And a curious cat came by and sniffed at her shoe.

The snowstorm lasted for two days. Then the sun came out and melted the snow.

Even then Amy didn't feel like going outside.

"Why don't you just go out for a little while?"
said Mama gently.

Amy went out. She wandered around. She sat on
the swing. She watched John playing nearby. Suddenly——

"Amy, Amy, come quick!"

What was John so excited about?

Run, Amy. Quickly.

Could it be?

It was. Sarah Jane!

But what had happened to her?

Her hair was muddy and matted.

Her paint was crumbled and cracked.

Worst of all, the elastic holding her arms and legs had broken. She had come apart completely.

"My poor baby!"

The children ran into the house with the broken doll. Maybe Mama would know how to fix Sarah Jane.

But Mama could not help.

How do you fix a broken doll?

An old doll made years and years ago.
Do you fix it with paint and paste?
With tape and glue?
Maybe she could not be fixed.
"Please don't throw her away," cried Amy.

"I remember reading once about a hospital for dolls..." That was Mama. Of course. That was it. A hospital. A special hospital just for broken dolls. They found an address in the telephone book.

They took the bus.

Then they walked.

It seemed like a very long trip to Amy, walking along with the poor broken doll in her arms.

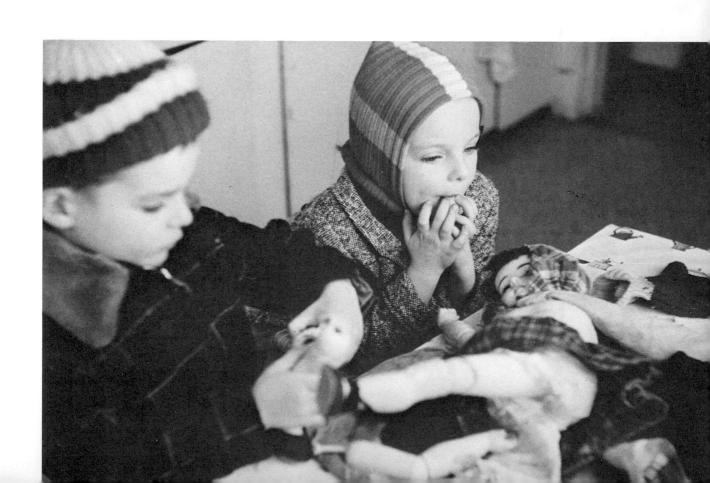

At last they were there.

"You wait outside," said Amy. "She's my child and I'd rather take care of her by myself."

So Mama and John waited outside.

"It doesn't look much like a hospital," thought Amy, as she opened the door.

Somewhere in the back a bell tinkled. But no one came. Amy put Sarah Jane down carefully on the counter.

"I'll just look around for a while."

Now Amy heard someone coming.

A tall man with a paint-stained shirt came from the back of the store.

"May I help you, young lady?"

Amy held Sarah Jane and showed him what had happened.

"Ah, yes, I see. What a shame! The legs, the arms, the paint. Ah, yes."

"But can you fix her?"

"I think I may be able to. But you will have to leave the doll here and come back Monday."

Monday. That was four days away.

It was a long time to wait.

Amy left Sarah Jane and went to tell Mama and John the news.

Monday had never taken such a long time to come.

When it finally arrived, Amy could hardly wait for school to be over. She hurried home and she and Mama went right over to the doll hospital.

They weren't quite finished with Sarah Jane. But the man invited Amy to come in and watch him work. Amy saw him put in the elastic that would hold her arms and legs. *Snap!* It went into place.

Sarah was whole again.

Her paint was new.

Her wig was clean.

She looked just the way she'd looked before.

Amy went home happily with her doll.

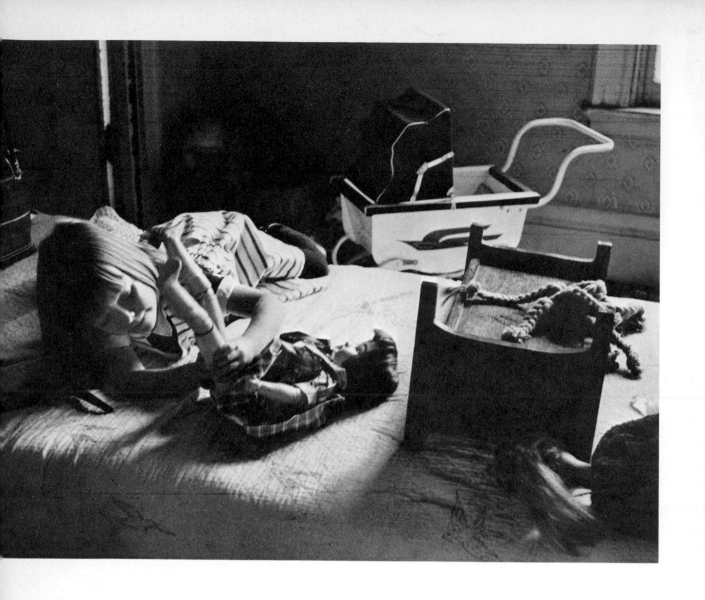

"What's the very nicest kind of celebration?"
Amy asked, happily undressing Sarah Jane.

"Well, I always like a wedding," said Mama.

"Then tomorrow we will have a wedding, to
celebrate Sarah Jane's coming home."

So the next day there was a wedding.

The bride looked beautiful.

And everyone lived happily ever after.